THIS SERIES OF BOOKS
IS DEDICATED TO THE MEMORY OF
ANNE-MARIE DALMAIS
WHOSE GREAT ENTHUSIASM
AND INSPIRATION MADE THIS
PROJECT COME TO LIFE

Four Little Friends

GYO FUJIKAWA
BE CAREFUL, BRIAN
BRIAN
and other tales

Modern Publishing
A Division of Unisystems, Inc.
New York, New York 10022
Printed in Italy

BE CAREFUL, BRIAN

Brian helped Sam fly his kite
On a windy day.
When Sam went home he left his toy
So Brian could still play.

The wind whipped 'round and 'round him.
Brian watched the kite soar up and down.
Then he tripped on something
And tumbled to the ground.

The kite took off without him.
Brian tried hard to catch up.
But the wind blew it away.
Brian knew he was out of luck.

Sam came running up the hill
Toward Brian, who felt bad.
He had to tell the truth and hope
That Sam would not be mad.

Sam knew his friend was sorry.
It was an accident.
Then the girls came by to say
They knew where Sam's kite went.

Off they ran to find the kite.
It was stuck in a tree.
Working all together,
The four friends got it free!

SAD SAM

When Sam is sad or lonely,
Rags tries to cheer him up.
Rags does the tricks Sam taught him;
He's one smart little pup!

Rags speaks, begs, and rolls over,
Sits up and shakes hands, too.
Soon Sam is smiling once again.
He's happy through and through.

When the show is over,
Rags gives his tail a wag.
Sam pats his head and tells him,
"You're my very best friend, Rags!"

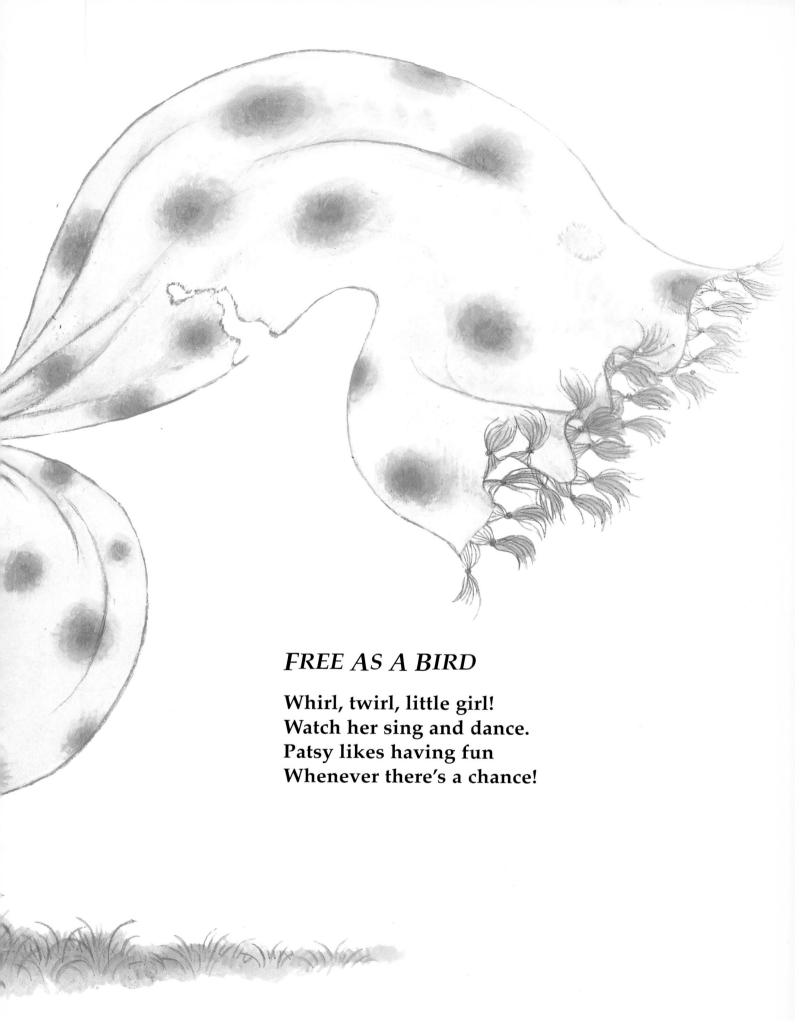

FREE AS A BIRD

Whirl, twirl, little girl!
Watch her sing and dance.
Patsy likes having fun
Whenever there's a chance!

BEARY BERRY SCARE

Four friends were in the woods one day
To go berry picking.
They took a basket and some pails.
Their fingers they were licking.

But when their pails were full, the friends
Heard noises coming near.
They hid behind a tree and saw
A baby bear appear!

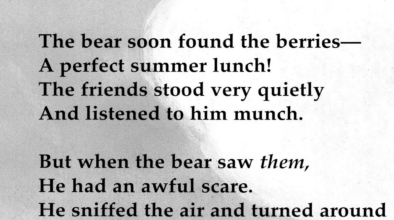

The bear soon found the berries—
A perfect summer lunch!
The friends stood very quietly
And listened to him munch.

But when the bear saw *them,*
He had an awful scare.
He sniffed the air and turned around
And ran off to his lair!